Don't Try This at Home!
Famous Daredevils

by

Meredith Phillips

SCHOLASTIC INC.
New York Toronto London Auckland
Sydney New Delhi Hong Kong

Cover
© Christophe Michot/Aurora Photos

Credits

p. 5: © Bernhard Spoettel/SNI/Reuters/Corbis; p. 6: © Bettmann/Corbis, tr: © Circus World Museum; p. 11: © Cornell Capa/Time Life Pictures/Getty Images; p. 12t: © Michael Ochs Archives/Getty Images, br: © Underwood & Underwood/Corbis; p. 18: © Harold A. Taylor Co./Smithsonian Institution, Washington, DC; p. 20: © AP Images, inset: © Press Association/AP Images; p. 27: © Ralph Crane/Time Life Pictures/Getty Images; p. 28: © Jean-Louis Blondeau/Polaris, inset: © Alan Welner/AP Images; p. 33: © Alan Welner/AP Images; p. 34: © Alexander Kensington; p. 39: © Brendon De Suza/iStockphoto; p. 40: © Cato Nordbakk; p. 44: © Christophe Michot/Aurora Photos

No part of this publication may be reproduced in whole or in part, or stored in a retrieval system, or transmitted in any form or by any means, electronic, mechanical, photocopying, recording, or otherwise, without written permission of the publisher. For information regarding permission, write to Scholastic Inc., 557 Broadway, New York, NY 10012.

Copyright © 2012 by Scholastic Inc.
All rights reserved. Published by Scholastic Inc.
Printed in the U.S.A.

ISBN-13: 978-0-545-31858-7
ISBN-10: 0-545-31858-0
(meets NASTA specifications)

SCHOLASTIC, READ 180, and associated logos are trademarks and/or registered trademarks of Scholastic Inc.
LEXILE is a registered trademark of MetaMetrics, Inc.

4 5 6 7 8 9 10   113   20 19 18 17 16 15 14 13 12 11

Contents

Introduction 4

**The Flying Zacchinis:
Human Cannonballs** 7

Bessie Coleman: Fearless Flyer 13

Evel Knievel: Maniac on a Motorcycle 21

Philippe Petit: Man on a Wire 29

Charon Henning: Nerves of Steel 35

Ana Isabel Dao: BASE Jumper 41

Glossary 45

Introduction

Most people try to stay out of danger. **Daredevils** go looking for it. Danger is their way of life!

What is a daredevil? It is someone who does extreme **stunts**. In this book, you will meet some of the world's great daredevils. One man shot his children from a cannon! A stunt pilot **thrilled** crowds with her flying tricks. A biker jumped huge distances on his motorcycle. He even tried to jump across a canyon!

BASE jumpers leap from the world's highest places. In this book, you will meet a jumper from Venezuela. She jumped from the highest waterfall on earth.

Why did these people become daredevils? Some grew up in a family of daredevils. They learned crazy tricks as kids. Others just liked the **excitement**. But all daredevils have one thing in common. They love to try the impossible. Often, they succeed.

Each daredevil has an amazing story. So fasten your seat belt and read on!

This BASE jumper just jumped from a mountain peak. It is 5,000 feet above ground. Is he brave—or just crazy?

Mario (*center*), Hugo (*left*), and Bruno Zacchini (*right*) pose next to their cannon. ➤

Hugo Zacchini flies from a cannon. This stunt took place in New York City.

> *"Flying isn't the hard part. Landing in the net is."* — Mario Zacchini

The Flying Zacchinis:
Human Cannonballs

The year is 1935. The U.S. is going through the **Great Depression**. It is a time of money trouble for many Americans. Some can't find jobs. Some can't afford food to eat.

People want to forget their troubles. So they go to shows, like the circus. (In 1935, there was no TV!)

At the circus, a band plays music. Then a truck drives in. A cannon is mounted on top. It looks like a big gun. But it won't shoot a cannonball. This cannon will shoot a man! Mario Zacchini, the human cannonball, will fly from this cannon!

Mario climbs onto the cannon. He drops down inside of it! Drums roll. The

audience holds its breath. The cannon **explodes**. It blasts Mario into the air! He flies across the arena. At last, he lands safely in a net on the other side.

A Circus Family

Mario Zacchini was born into circus life. He and his eight brothers and sisters grew up in Italy. Their father, Ildebrando, ran a circus.

One day, Ildebrando saw a circus act he liked. A big lever sent a man flying through the air. The man landed in a net.

Ildebrando wondered how to make the act better. Flying through the air was exciting. Getting *shot* through the air would be more exciting! Ildebrando decided to shoot someone from a cannon.

Who could he shoot? The answer was simple: his children, of course!

The Zacchinis built their first cannon in 1922. Mario's brother Hugo was the first human cannonball. But nearly everyone in the family got into the act. Sometimes Mario's two sisters **performed**. They flew from the cannon together.

Taking the Act to America

In 1929, the family performed in Denmark. A man named John Ringling saw their act. He loved it! Ringling ran a circus in the U.S. He hired the family. They came to the U.S. They joined the Ringling Brothers' Circus. Crowds loved the Flying Zacchinis!

Mario became the most famous Zacchini. For years, he flew from a cannon. He did it three times a day! He went as fast as 90 miles per hour. "Flying isn't the hard part. Landing in the net is," he said.

Mario told stories about his stunts. "One time, we tested the cannon. We used a dummy that weighed the same as me," he said. But the dummy went *over* the net.

It landed in the ocean. The testers couldn't find it. Mario got worried. "Are they going to be able to find me?" he wondered.

The Zacchinis' Final Acts

The Zacchinis never got lost in the ocean. But they *did* get hurt sometimes. Some siblings broke bones. Others banged their heads. Sometimes, they got knocked out. Even so, the Zacchinis kept flying.

In 1940, a cannon shot Mario over a Ferris wheel. He landed wrong in the net. He broke his spine. He broke a shoulder and some ribs, too. Mario **recovered**. He lived to be 87 years old. But he never flew out of a cannon again.

Still, the family kept the act going for many years. Mario's nephew Hugo was the last Zacchini in the business. His last flight was in 1991. This family will be remembered as the world's most famous human cannonballs.

How can a person survive a cannon blast?

Most cannons shoot huge lead balls. It takes lots of power to blast something so heavy. Usually, people use gunpowder. But how could a human survive that?

The truth is simple. Even a Zacchini could *not* survive a gunpowder blast. So, how did the family do it?

Gunpowder did not power the cannon. Air did! The Zacchinis put a platform inside the cannon. A "human cannonball" stood on the platform. Then a blast of pressurized air pushed the platform upward. The blast shot the person across a long distance.

The family tricked their audience. They lit gunpowder *near* the cannon. It made a lot of smoke and noise. People thought gunpowder powered the cannon.

Bessie Coleman was the first African-American woman to get a pilot's license.

"I would not take no for an answer."
— Bessie Coleman

Bessie Coleman:
Fearless Flyer

Stunt pilot Bessie Coleman was a flying daredevil. People called her Queen Bess. She ruled the sky with her stunts. She flew her plane in loops, rolls, and nosedives.

Bessie got famous in the 1920s. Her success was especially amazing for that time. She was African American. And in her day, black people did not have equal rights. She had to fight **prejudice** to fly.

A Rough Start

Bessie Coleman was born in Texas in 1892. Her grandparents were slaves. Her parents were poor farmers. They could not read or write. Bessie's school was for black students only. It did not have as many books or supplies as schools for white students. The school stopped after eighth grade. Bessie's area had no high school for black students.

Bessie loved school. She was a good student. At night, she read to her family. She said that one day she would be someone important.

As a young woman, Bessie went to college. But she ran out of money after one year. She went home. She washed clothes to earn money. She wanted a better life.

First Chicago, Then the World

In 1915, Bessie moved to Chicago. She got a job at a barbershop. A huge war was going on in Europe. It is now known as World War I. Some of Bessie's customers flew planes in the war. She loved hearing their stories.

Airplanes were a recent **invention**. The first flight was in 1903. Bessie learned that some pilots were women. She wanted to fly, too.

U.S. flight schools would not teach an African-American woman. Bessie heard that France was different. Prejudice wasn't as strong there. In 1920, she moved to Paris. She became the first African-American woman to get a pilot's license.

Now she needed a job. Airlines did not exist in 1920. People traveled long distances by train or boat. So there were few jobs for pilots. Some pilots put on air shows to make a living. Bessie learned how to do flying tricks. Then she went back to America. She was ready to perform.

Queen of the Sky

Bessie Coleman flew in her first air show in 1922. She was an instant success. People called her "the world's greatest woman flier." She thrilled large crowds.

How did she do it? Bessie took off in

her plane. She flew her plane in "loop-de-loops." Those are big circles. At the top of each circle, her plane was upside down! She also did "figure eights." She flew around in the shape of an 8. People got dizzy just watching!

Then Bessie did something even more daring. She flew straight toward the ground. It looked like she would crash! At the last second, she pulled up. The crowd was always shocked.

Bessie used her fame to help other African Americans. **Segregation** existed in many towns. The best schools were for whites only. The best hotels and restaurants were, too. Blacks could not sit with whites in theaters. They could not sit near whites in train stations.

Some air shows had separate entrances for blacks and whites. Bessie would not fly in those shows. She would not fly unless blacks and whites could enter together.

Bessie had a plan. She wanted to open a flying school. She would teach African Americans. Sadly, she did not make it happen. She did not live long enough.

Death of a Daredevil

Bessie lived like a daredevil. She died like a daredevil, too. On April 30, 1926, she fell from a plane. Bessie wanted to parachute from the plane. She was planning how to do it. Another pilot was flying. He lost control. Bessie was thrown 500 feet to her death. She was just 34 years old.

More than 15,000 people went to the funeral. Bessie Coleman still inspires people today. She is a role model to anyone who has a dream that seems impossible.

> *What qualities do you think a person needed to be a successful barnstormer?*

The History of Barnstorming

A big war—World War I—ended in 1918. After the war, the U.S. military didn't need all of its war planes. The military sold planes cheaply. Pilots bought them. They did flying tricks for the public. People called the pilots **barnstormers**. That's because they often held air shows on farms.

Barnstorming was dangerous. This man fell from a plane in 1920. He was trying to make an airplane-to-automobile transfer.

Come One, Come All!

Barnstorming shows were popular in the 1920s. A group of pilots would arrive at a farm. They paid the owner to use the land. Then they flew over the town. They dropped flyers telling about the show. People would find the flyers. Big crowds showed up at the farm. They paid to watch the show.

Barnstorming was a thrilling way to make a living. Pilots flew their planes in crazy ways. They did spins and dives. They did figure eights. They flew in big loop-de-loops. People called **aerialists** went on top of the wings. They did tricks. Sometimes they danced or played tennis. Sometimes they even jumped from one plane to another!

When the show was over, the pilots moved on. They flew from place to place. They put on air shows across the United States.

The End of an Era

There were few rules about **aviation** safety back then. Many barnstormers were hurt or killed. In 1927, the government passed new **regulations**. Flying got safer. But the barnstorming era ended.

In 1974, Evel Knievel jumped over seven Mack trucks in Toronto, Canada.

Evel flies over 13 buses.

"Who would wanna take a motorcycle and jump it over these obstacles, miss them, and keep getting up and doing it over and over again?"
— Evel Knievel

Evel Knievel:
Maniac on a Motorcycle

The year is 1965. A man stands outside a motorcycle shop. It's an **ordinary** shop. Yet the man is no ordinary man. And he is doing something very odd. He is lining up boxes of snakes. Next to him, there is a mountain lion in a cage!

The man is about to do a stunt. He will try to leap *over* the animals. And he will do it on a motorcycle!

He gets on his cycle. The engine roars. He zooms up a ramp. He flies into the air. Twenty feet of snakes and lion are below him. Will he make it across?

The motorcycle bounces back to earth. The jump is a success!

In 1965, the man was unknown. But soon, everyone would know his name.

Becoming Evel Knievel

Who was that crazy daredevil? His name was Robert Craig Knievel. He became famous as Evel Knievel. But as a boy, he was just called Bobby.

Bobby was born in Butte, Montana, in 1938. As a kid, he did tricks on his bicycle. He kept doing stunts when he got older. He even did them at work.

Bobby had a job driving a big machine. He was paid to dig up soil. But one day, he "popped a wheelie." He tilted the machine onto its back wheels! The machine hit a power line. The city of Butte went dark.

Bobby got arrested for that stunt. Later, he got into more trouble. He spent time in jail. A jailer gave him a nickname: Evil.

It means wicked and bad! The name rhymes with Knievel. Bobby liked that. Yet, he didn't want to call himself evil. So he changed the spelling. He spelled his new name "Evel."

Evel got fired from his machine job. He had many jobs after that. He entered ski jumping contests. He started a hockey team! He sold motorcycles, too. At that job, he arm-wrestled with customers. What happened if they won? Evel gave them a $100 **discount**.

Evel didn't just sell motorcycles. He rode them, too. He learned to do a wheelie. He rode his motorcycle with the front wheel up in the air! He also learned to ride while standing on the seat. He started doing motorcycle stunts. He never stopped.

Making History One Jump at a Time

Evel formed a group of stunt riders. He called them Evel Knievel and His

Motorcycle Daredevils. They did their first show in 1966. It was a big success!

Then Evel got hurt. His group broke up. Later, Evel began to perform solo. He traveled from town to town.

Evel started jumping over cars. In Canada, he set a world record. He flew over 19 cars. In California, he jumped over 50 cars. That was another world record. In Ohio, Evel tried to jump over 14 buses. But he landed on the last bus. He still broke a record.

People loved Evel's act! He became a TV star. He made many jumps on live TV. Millions of fans watched.

Evel Knievel made about 300 jumps in his career. He broke many records. He broke many bones, too! In 1972, he had 471 **fractures**. In 1973, he broke his skull. The blow knocked him out. He did not wake up for 29 days.

Snake River Canyon

Evel's injuries rarely stopped him for long. In fact, he kept planning bigger jumps. Evel wanted to jump across a canyon! It is called Snake River Canyon. It is in Idaho, in the western United States. The canyon is a quarter of a mile wide.

On September 8, 1974, Evel arrived at the canyon. TV cameras were there to film his jump. Evel wore his usual costume. It was a white jumpsuit. It had stars and stripes, like the American flag.

Evel had a special motorcycle for this jump. It was powered by rocket engines! Its nose pointed up in the air. The cycle even looked like a rocket.

At 3:36 P.M., Evel soared into the sky. A parachute flew out behind his cycle. But the parachute opened too soon!

Evel almost made it to the other side. Then, the parachute pulled him down. It pulled him into the canyon. Evel crashed at the bottom. Yet, somehow, he was not badly hurt!

A Daredevil Retires

Evel Knievel stopped jumping in 1980. He was only 41 years old. But his body was in bad shape. His many crashes had caused lasting damage.

People often asked Evel about his career. Why did he risk his life over and over? Even Evel was not sure!

"Who would wanna [do that]?" he wondered. "I don't know why. It's something inside of a man that drives him. I hope I find out what the reason is."

> *Would you like to watch Evel's stunts? Why or why not?*

Breaking Records With Broken Bones

Evel Knievel still holds the world record for most broken bones. He broke 35 different bones in his body!

Philippe Petit walked on a wire more than 1,000 feet in the air. He did not use a safety net!

*"When I see three oranges, I juggle.
When I see two towers, I walk."*
— Philippe Petit

Philippe Petit:
Man on a Wire

Philippe Petit was born in France in 1949. He started doing stunts as a teenager. He walked a **tightrope**. He juggled. He rode a unicycle. He performed on the streets of Paris, France.

In 1968, Philippe read a magazine article. It told about two tall buildings. They were called the Twin Towers. They were in New York City. They were part of the World Trade Center.

In 2001, terrorists destroyed the buildings. But in 1968, the Twin Towers were still being built.

Philippe kept thinking about the towers. He had a wild idea. He wanted to run a wire from one tower to the other. Then he would walk across it!

A Man With a Plan

Does walking between the towers sound crazy? It was! Those towers were 110 stories tall. They were more than 1,000 feet high. They were the tallest buildings in the world!

Still, Philippe's mind was made up. He began to prepare. He practiced all the time. He walked in other crazy places! In 1971, he strung a wire on a cathedral in Paris. It was over 225 feet high! He walked back and forth. Crowds watched in awe.

In 1973, Philippe went to Sydney, Australia. He visited a high bridge. He strung a tightrope on it. The wire was 300 feet high. Philippe did tricks up there!

Philippe never used a safety net. But he planned his stunts for months or years. He said his planning was the only safety net he needed. "My safety net is much stronger than anything else in the world," he claimed.

The Planning Continues

Philippe spent years planning the Twin Towers stunt. He made trips to New York. He visited the towers. He pretended he was working in the buildings. He sneaked up to the roof! (Back then, building security was not very strict.)

Philippe studied the towers. Winds high up are strong. Tall buildings need "give." They have to sway a little in the wind. If they don't, wind can damage them. Philippe saw how the towers moved. He planned what kind of wire to use.

By August 7, 1974, Philippe was ready. The night before, he and his crew sneaked on top of the towers. They strung a 450-pound wire between the buildings.

A Walk in the Sky

At 7:15 A.M., Philippe stepped onto the wire. He walked back and forth. He danced. He sat down. He even lay down on the wire! One slip, and Philippe would die. But he was having the time of his life.

People on the ground spotted Philippe. They could not believe their eyes! Police raced to the tops of the towers. They tried to stop Philippe. He just teased them! He walked close. Then he backed away. After 45 minutes, he finally got off the wire.

The police arrested Philippe. But he did not go to jail. His walk was big news. People loved him! Instead of jail, Philippe did tricks. He performed for kids in New York City.

The Twin Towers no longer exist. But New Yorkers will always remember them—and the amazing daredevil who walked between them.

Physics and Tightrope Walking

It can be hard to balance on a tightrope. Tightrope walkers use the rules of **physics** to help them.

The force of gravity pulls us down. When you walk on a wire, a tiny movement can make you lose your balance.

A balancing pole spreads out a person's weight. It takes bigger movements to make you fall. If you start to fall left, you can move the pole a bit to the right. That will help you balance.

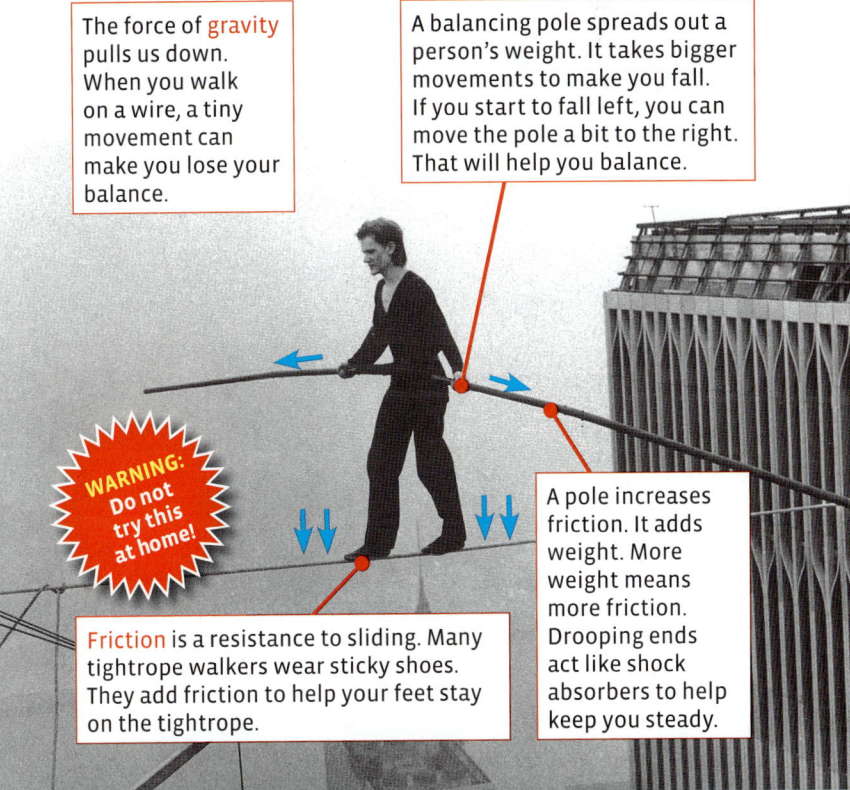

WARNING: Do not try this at home!

A pole increases friction. It adds weight. More weight means more friction. Drooping ends act like shock absorbers to help keep you steady.

Friction is a resistance to sliding. Many tightrope walkers wear sticky shoes. They add friction to help your feet stay on the tightrope.

Charon Henning swallows a sword!

"Charon Henning ... is the smoothest steel dropper you'll find anywhere."

— James Taylor, Editor,
Shocked & Amazed! magazine

Charon Henning: *Nerves of Steel*

It's a warm afternoon in southern Florida. Sunlight sparkles on the fairgrounds. A scary act is about to begin. A man introduces Charon Henning. She is a sword swallower.

Charon holds up a shiny sword. She puts it in her mouth. She tilts her head. She slides the sword down her throat. She slides it deeper. It goes into her stomach. Only the handle can be seen.

Charon takes a bow. The sword is still in her body! Carefully, she slides it out.

Real or Fake?

Do performers like Charon *really* swallow swords? Or do they fake it? You might think they are faking. Wrong!

Sword swallowing is an ancient art. People have done it for thousands of years. And it is not fake.

Still, sword swallowers don't truly swallow. When you swallow, you close your throat. You tighten the muscles. You push food down. Sword swallowers open their throats. Then they slide the sword in.

This trick is *very dangerous*. A sword can tear up your body. It can kill you fast!

Learning Her Craft

Charon grew up in Maryland. As a teen, she did puppet shows and plays. Later, she discovered sword swallowing.

Charon learned to swallow swords from Red Stuart. He is an expert. He can swallow 50 swords at once!

It takes time to learn such a dangerous skill. Charon trained for many months. She learned to stand very straight. She learned to keep her body still, too.

"My swords are not sharp," she says. "But they can still harm me. I need to be very careful."

A Busy Life

Charon performs at circuses and fairs. She does many shows a day. She swallows three or four swords in each show. Once she worked for 14 hours straight. She swallowed a sword 80 or 90 times!

She has to stay in shape. "I do yoga to stretch out my body," she says. She also eats well.

Charon Henning is one of the only female sword swallowers in the world. Swallowing swords isn't for everyone. But it suits her perfectly.

An Interview With Charon Henning

Q: What's the best part of your job?

A: *It's when girls tell me my show was the best thing they've seen. Then I know I have done my job. I have done something important. Something may look impossible. But practice and a good teacher will make it possible. I want people to know that. Hard work and practice are the most important things.*

Q: What was your scariest moment as a sword swallower?

A: *I am scared every time I swallow a sword. It is an incredibly dangerous thing to do.*

My scariest moment was when I hurt myself during a show. A very heavy sword poked a hole in my throat. My audience had no idea. Neither did I!

Then I coughed up blood. A friend took me to the nearest E.R. Two hours later I was in terrible pain. I had surgery to save my life. I ate through a tube for a week. I spent three months recovering. Then I could swallow a sword again. I've been fine ever since.

Q: Do you always use the same sword?

A: *I use five swords. I make sure they are smooth, with no sharp edges. Then they are as safe as possible to use. I clean them before and after every show.*

Q: Do you travel a lot? Where do you live?

A: *I travel full-time. I live in a trailer. I see the country. I meet people from all walks of life.*

I have a partner named Alex. He also swallows swords. We work together all over the country.

I sew all of our costumes. I sew for other performers as well. When I'm not performing, I draw a lot. I also enjoy hiking, reading, old movies, and cooking.

In 2009, Ana Isabel Dao jumped from the world's highest waterfall.

> *"BASE jumping has taken me to incredible places."*
> — Ana Isabel Dao

Ana Isabel Dao: *BASE Jumper*

BASE jumping is an extreme sport. It's all about jumping from high places.

Why is it called BASE jumping? You must jump from four things to become a real BASE jumper. You have to jump off a building and a high antenna. You have to jump off a span. (That's another name for "bridge.") You must also jump from a part of earth (such as a cliff).

Building. **A**ntenna. **S**pan. **E**arth. The first letters spell BASE.

BASE jumpers use a parachute. Still, this sport is very dangerous. That's one reason Ana Isabel Dao loves it.

A Family Tradition

Ana grew up with a daredevil dad. They are from Venezuela. The highest waterfall in the world is there. It's called Angel Falls. It is 20 times higher than Niagara Falls. In 1983, Ana's dad jumped from Angel Falls.

Ana was just two years old then. Years later, she and her father jumped from Angel Falls together. But Ana was always a daredevil.

"It's in my character," she said. "When I was little, I was a real menace! I am still hyper. I can't be quiet for long."

Ana began to **skydive** at age 16. In 2005, two friends invited her on a BASE jumping course. She jumped off a bridge.

"I felt scared!" she said. "But I really wanted to do it! Once I did, it felt great. I have never looked back. BASE jumping has taken me to incredible places. I have met great people from around the world."

Angel Falls—and Beyond

In 2006, Ana became the first Venezuelan woman to jump from Angel Falls. In 2008, she and two other women made a plan. They would all jump from Angel Falls.

Angel Falls is in the jungle. The women hiked for six days to get there. Then they prepared for the jump. They wore "wingsuits." The suits have fabric between the legs. More fabric is under the arms. The fabric gives jumpers better control. Each woman had a parachute, too.

At last they were ready. Months of planning ended in 20 seconds of free fall. Landing was hard. There is just one clear space below the falls. Still, all three women landed safely!

Ana lives in France now. She is a lawyer. Her work is exciting. But she still goes BASE jumping for some extra thrills.

All BASE jumpers must jump from at least one building. This one is 1,351 feet high.

Glossary

aerialists *(noun)*: people who perform tricks high in the air

audience *(noun)*: a group of people who watch a performance

aviation *(noun)*: the flying of planes and other aircraft

barnstormers *(noun)*: 1920s stunt pilots who traveled doing air shows

daredevils *(noun)*: people who do very risky tricks

discount *(noun)*: an amount of money that is taken off the price of something

excitement *(noun)*: intense enjoyment

explodes *(verb)*: bursts or blows to bits

fractures *(noun)*: breaks in bones

Great Depression *(noun)*: a period of hard times from 1929 through the 1930s, when many people could not find jobs

invention *(noun)*: something new that didn't exist before

ordinary *(adjective)*: common or usual

performed *(verb)*: put on a show for people

physics *(noun)*: the science of how things move

prejudice *(noun)*: a negative idea about someone that isn't based on facts

recovered *(verb)*: got better after being hurt or sick

regulations *(noun)*: rules or laws

segregation *(noun)*: the practice of keeping different races apart

skydive *(verb)*: to jump from a plane and land by parachute

stunts *(noun)*: dangerous tricks

thrilled *(verb)*: got someone excited

tightrope *(noun)*: a rope or wire stretched high in the air, for walking and doing tricks